In My Backyard

In My Backyard

John DeVries

Werner Zimmermann

Scholastic Canada Ltd.

Scholastic Canada Ltd.
175 Hillmount Road, Markham, Ontario, Canada L6C 1Z7

Scholastic Inc.
555 Broadway, New York, NY 10012, USA

Scholastic Australia Pty Limited
PO Box 579, Gosford, NSW 2250, Australia

Scholastic New Zealand Limited
Private Bag 94407, Greenmount, Auckland, New Zealand

Scholastic Ltd.
Villiers House, Clarendon Avenue, Leamington Spa,
Warwickshire CV32 5PR, UK

7 6 5 4 3 2 1   Printed in Canada   02 03 04 05 06

National Library of Canada Cataloguing in Publication Data

De Vries, John
  In my backyard

For the sole use of the Government of Ontario.
ISBN 0-7791-1367-5

I. Zimmermann, H. Werner (Heinz Werner), 1951- II. Title.

PS8557.E89I5 2002   jC813'.54   C2001-930711-9
PZ7.D48In 2002

To Wanita
John

To Mupps, all heart and understanding.
And to Klaus, without whose frog this book
could not have been.
Werner

In my backyard I have a frog.

2

My mother found him on a log.

3

I called my frog my good friend Jim.

My mummy yelled, "Get rid of him!"

I asked my dad if Jim could stay.

My daddy said, "Take him away!"

7

I asked my grandpa if I could keep . . .

9

Oh, he's asleep.

10

I showed my sister my good friend Jim.
She nearly ran right over him!

13

So!
I told my dog (his name is Rover)

that he would soon be moving over.

15

And now Jim lives
with my dog in his house

with his cat and my mouse

17

with his bowl and my pail

with his box and my nail

with his rope and my ring

with his ball and my string

with his rug and my coat

with his tub and my boat

23

with his rod and my reel

with his rake and my wheel

25

with his pole and my flag

with his hole in my bag.

27

Rover, you're a pal!